CW00838767

Mosé
MOUSE
& Friends!

Freddy Frog's
Rotten Day!

Freddy Frog's rotten day!

Freddy the Frog opened his eyes,
gave a big stretch and a yawn.

YAWNNN

To his surprise he was tumbling fast,
no longer safe on the lawn.

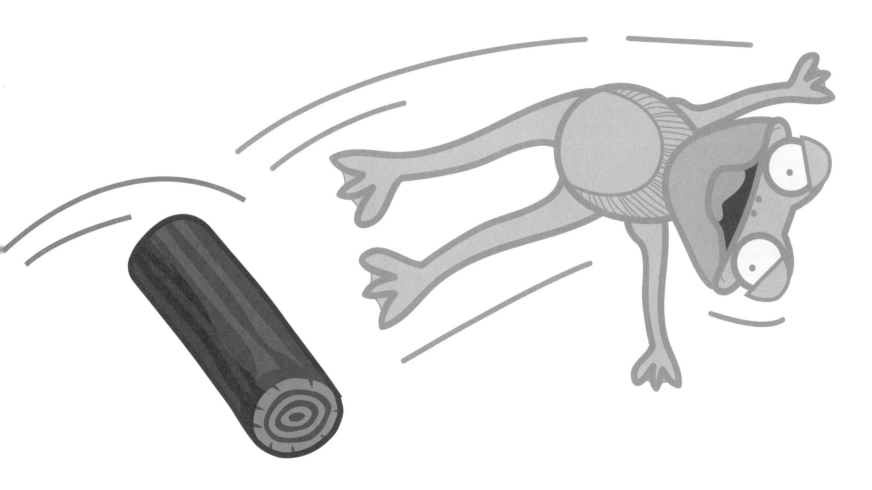

His log had rolled and he fell with a **SPLASH** into the water so cold.

Feeling hungry and wet he thought breakfast was best,
but his food was all covered in mould!

Freddy jumped up with a **GRUMBLING** tummy,
he was in such a terrible mood.

"What a horrible start to my morning," he thought, and went on the hunt for some food.

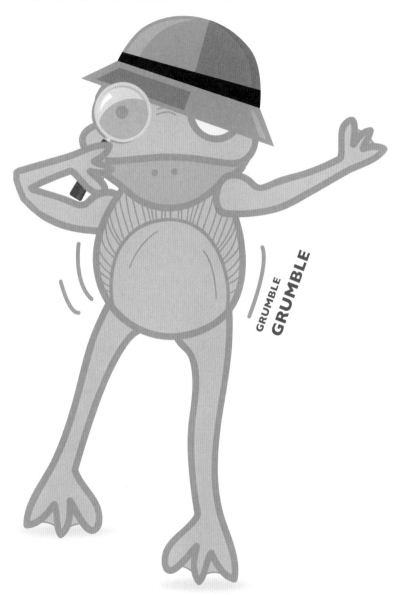

Feeling so sad, he decided to find,
Mosé Mouse to put a smile on his face.

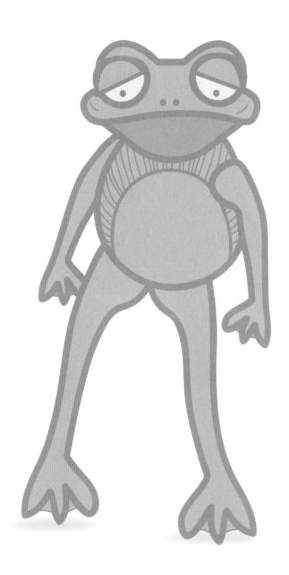

His best **best** **BEST** friend in the whole wide world, who no-one could ever replace.

All of a sudden, Sebastian appeared,
leaping down from his tree in a rush.

He made Freddy jump and he fell
with a **BUMP**,
as Sebastian scampered into a bush.

"You scared me Sebastian!" Freddy
shouted, upset.
"That wasn't very nice of you,"

I need to find Mosé, my best **best *BEST*** friend,
he'll know just what to do.

Next Freddy bumped into Maisie the Mole,
eating bugs and flies for her lunch.

She gobbled them quick, turned to Freddy and shrugged,
"Sorry Freddy, there's none left to **MUNCH!"**

Well, poor Freddy felt worse than ever,
he needed his best friend and quick!

But while searching the farmyard for Mosé Mouse,
he came across Chicken the Chick.

"Hello Freddy!" said Chicken with a warm sunny smile,
"Would you like to see some of my magic?"

"I really do think it might cheer you up and stop you from looking so tragic."

Chicken pulled out of his magic hat,
the **JUICIEST** bug by far.

He passed it to Freddy who gobbled it down, shouting -

"Chicken, you **SUPERSTAR!**"

GOBBLE GOBBLE

Freddy began to feel better,
with his tummy all full to the brim.

He turned his frown upside down,
and his grimace turned into a **GRIN!**

Just at that moment, who should appear,
but Mosé Mouse whistling a tune.

"Mosé my friend!" Freddy exclaimed,
"My day has been so full of gloom!"

"But Chicken the Chick did a smart magic trick, and he shared with me his food,"

His one act of **KINDNESS** turned my day around,
and now I'm in such a good mood!"

Mosé gave Freddy a hug and high-five,
as the friends went to play in the wood.

Showing **KINDNESS** and **LOVE**
can overcome all,
and turn any rotten day into good!